Dear Parent:
Your child's love of reading starts here!

Every child learns to read in a different way and at his or her own speed. Some go back and forth between reading levels and read favorite books again and again. Others read through each level in order. You can help your young reader improve and become more confident by encouraging his or her own interests and abilities. From books your child reads with you to the first books he or she reads alone, there are I Can Read Books for every stage of reading:

SHARED READING
Basic language, word repetition, and whimsical illustrations, ideal for sharing with your emergent reader

BEGINNING READING
Short sentences, familiar words, and simple concepts for children eager to read on their own

READING WITH HELP
Engaging stories, longer sentences, and language play for developing readers

READING ALONE
Complex plots, challenging vocabulary, and high-interest topics for the independent reader

ADVANCED READING
Short paragraphs, chapters, and exciting themes for the perfect bridge to chapter books

I Can Read Books have introduced children to the joy of reading since 1957. Featuring award-winning authors and illustrators and a fabulous cast of beloved characters, I Can Read Books set the standard for beginning readers.

A lifetime of discovery begins with the magical words **"I Can Read!"**

Visit www.icanread.com for information
on enriching your child's reading experience.

*To all the new members of
our lucky family, with love.
—K.K.*

*For my unconventional and
loving parents, Robert and
Julie Carter.
—A.C.*

I Can Read Book® is a trademark of HarperCollins Publishers.

The Best Seat in Kindergarten
Text copyright © 2019 by Katharine Kenah
Illustrations copyright © 2019 by Abby Carter

Library of Congress Control Number: 2018938258
ISBN 978-0-06-268641-1 (trade bdg.)—ISBN 978-0-06-268640-4 (pbk.)

Book design by Celeste Knudsen

19 20 21 22 23 SCP 10 9 8 7 6 5 4 3 2 1   ❖   First Edition

The
BEST SEAT
in Kindergarten

story by Katharine Kenah
pictures by Abby Carter

HARPER
An Imprint of HarperCollinsPublishers

It was the first day
of kindergarten.
Everyone was new at school.

Sam did not know anyone.

No one knew where to sit.

"It's beautiful outside,"
said Sam's teacher, Ms. Tate.
"Let's take a nature walk."

Ms. Tate passed out paper bags.
"Find something interesting.
Then show us what you found."

Sophie looked for rocks.

Sam found a rock for Sophie.

"Thank you, Sam!" said Sophie.

Miguel looked for bugs.

Sam found a bug for Miguel.

"Thank you, Sam!" said Miguel.

Lily looked for pinecones.

Sam found a pinecone for Lily.

"Thank you, Sam!" said Lily.

Ollie looked for flowers.

Sam found flowers for Ollie.

"Thank you, Sam!" said Ollie.

Nina looked for acorns.

Sam found acorns for Nina.

"Thank you, Sam!" said Nina.

"Time to go," said Ms. Tate.
The kindergarteners walked
back to school
with their teacher.

When everyone was sitting,
Ms. Tate said,
"Show us what you found."

"I found rocks," said Sophie.

"Sam helped me," said Sophie.

"I found bugs," said Miguel.

ers," said Ollie.

"Sam helped me," said Miguel.

23

"I found pinecones," said Lily.

"I found flowe

"Sam helped me," said Ollie.

"I found acorns," said Nina.

"Sam helped me," said Nina.

Sam's bag was empty.

"What did you find, Sam?"

asked Ms. Tate.

"Friends!" said Sam.

Sam had the best seat
in kindergarten.
Sam sat with his friends.